S.C. Waite

Graceful Riding

Anatiposi

S.C. Waite

Graceful Riding

Reprint of the original, first published in 1859.

1st Edition 2023 | ISBN: 978-3-38231-204-6

Anatiposi Verlag is an imprint of Outlook Verlagsgesellschaft mbH.

Verlag (Publisher): Outlook Verlag GmbH, Zeilweg 44, 60439 Frankfurt, Deutschland
Vertretungsberechtigt (Authorized to represent): E. Roepke, Zeilweg 44, 60439 Frankfurt, Deutschland
Druck (Print): Books on Demand GmbH, In de Tarpen 42, 22848 Norderstedt, Deutschland

GRACEFUL RIDING.

A

POCKET MANUAL FOR EQUESTRIANS.

ABRIDGED AND REVISED FROM "WAITE'S EQUESTRIAN'S MANUAL,"

DEDICATED TO H.R.H. PRINCE ALBERT.

BY

S. C. WAITE, ESQ.

LONDON:

ROBERT HARDWICKE, 192, PICCADILLY:

AND ALL BOOKSELLERS.

1859.

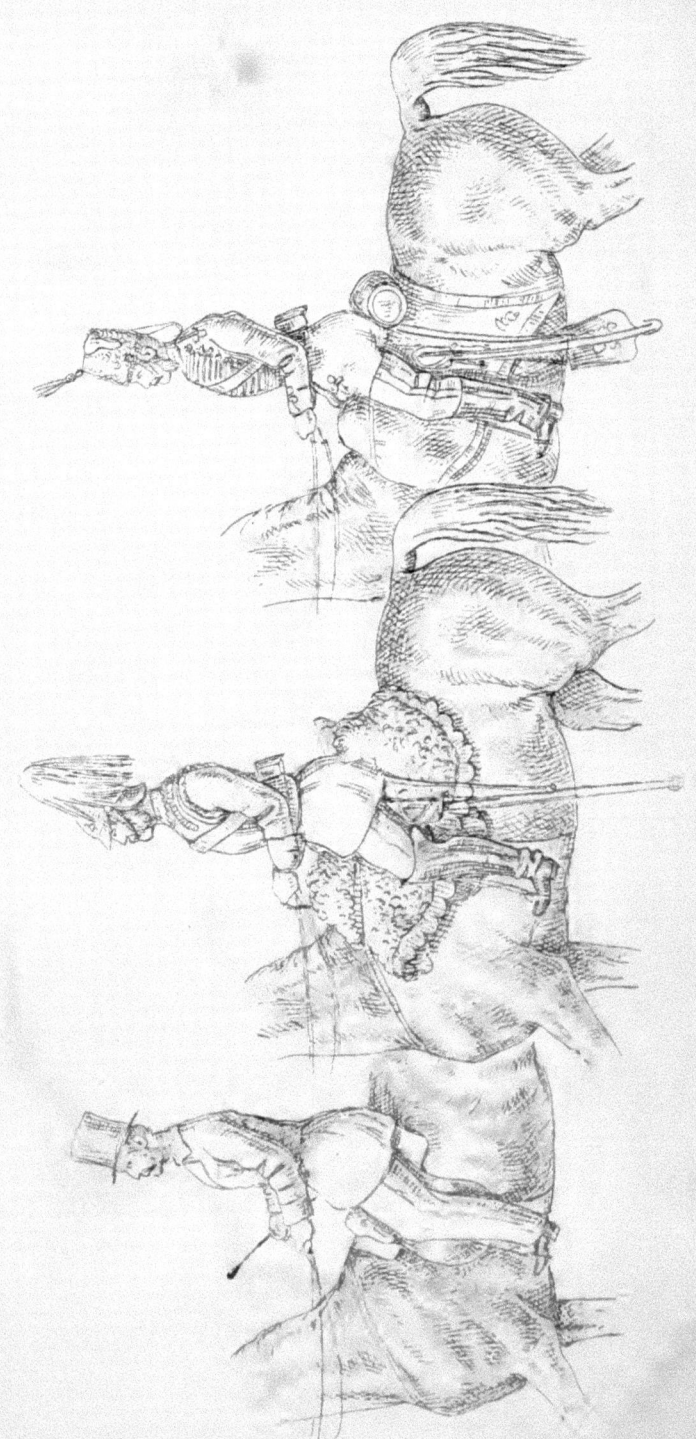

Graceful Riding

A

Pocket Manual

For Equestrians.

BY S. C. WAITE Esqre.

London,

ROBERT HARDWICKE 192 Piccadilly

AND ALL BOOKSELLERS.

PREFACE.

THE Author's last publication, " The Equestrian's Manual," having met with so kind a reception from the Press and the Public—one which he looks upon with the greatest gratitude—has induced him to compile for the use of Equestrians of both sexes the present little Work, in the sincere hope that his humble efforts may, in some degree, aid in obviating the many severe and often fatal accidents, the result, in most instances, of inexperience in Horsemanship.

Should he have attained this end, and given some instruction to the nervous and timid, or *any* to the experienced equestrian, he will feel himself well repaid.

INTRODUCTION.

THE science of Equitation has for many years been allowed, by the testimony and strong recommendation of the most eminent of the faculty, to be an accomplishment highly conducive and most beneficial to health ; assisting the blood in its proper circulation through the frame, on which depends wholly good spirits, and freedom from bilious, hypochondriacal, and nervous affections.

Parents should not neglect to have imparted to their children an art so calculated for the development of grace and beauty in maturity, and, above all other considerations, *one* that so eminently guards against the many diseases of this varying climate ; diseases which are, in fact, almost, if we may use the term, "indigenous" to the spring and summer of life.

Physicians, of the past and present time, whose mere names should be sufficient to procure every patronage, are in favour of the acquirement of this most essential and elegant science. The skill necessary to become a perfect rider, can only be obtained through the tuition of a first-rate master ; and, as far as the accomplishment can be explained within the limits of a book, the Author has endeavoured to do so ; but he repeats there is much which cannot be written, and is only to be acquired through personal tuition.

Lessons in the school *alone* can seldom make a good rider. In it the horse and the pupil become accustomed to the same monotonous routine day after day ; but when they emerge on the road it is found that the expert rider of the *school* is deficient in tact and skill ; and, in fact, has learnt but little. The nature of the animal will occasion this ; changing the scene of every-day objects in the school, for the great variety he must meet on the road, gives an impetus to his hitherto dormant spirit ; then the rider will find that he must exert all the skill and judgment he possesses to keep his horse under the proper control indispensable to his safe guidance.

In conclusion, should this work contribute to the enlightenment of ladies and gentlemen desirous of becoming *finished equestrians*, it will have accomplished the end for which it was undertaken.

DESCRIPTION OF PLATES.

PLATE I.

The first figure represents WAITE'S IMPROVED SEAT.

The position is on the same system as the Cavalry, but being more *négligé* in appearance, and much less constrained in feeling, although equally correct, imparts a more elegant and graceful seat to the rider.

HEAVY DRAGOON.

HUSSAR.

PLATE II.

RACING.

HUNTING.

PARK.

PLATE III.

The first figure represents the GENERAL SEAT of Ladies on their saddles.

The second shows the position of a Lady when mounted

according to Mr. WAITE'S METHOD of tuition ; by it a firm seat is gained on the saddle, and consequently it is more secure than the usual seat ; being also more graceful and elegant in appearance, and giving the rider a superior command over her horse, and obviating the danger of the habit-skirt becoming entangled in the horse's legs.

PART I.

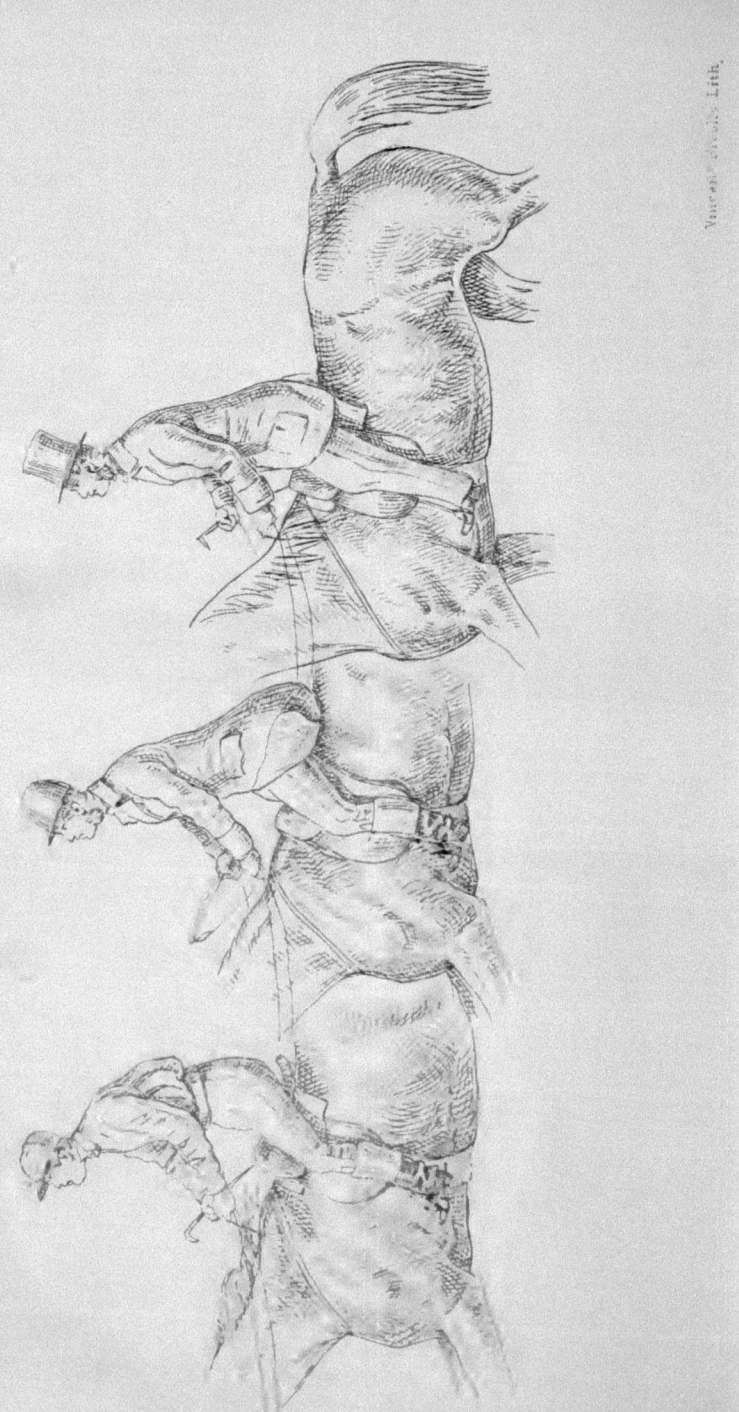

CHARACTER AND MANAGEMENT OF THE HORSE, WITH DIRECTIONS FOR RIDING.

A KNOWLEDGE of the general character and disposition of the horse is really and absolutely necessary to his skilful management, from his extremely nervous sensibility, his aptness to take the various impressions of fear, affection, or dislike, to any of which he is naturally very quickly disposed.

> " Reas'ning at ev'ry step he treads,
> Man yet mistakes his way ;
> While meaner things by instinct led
> Are rarely known to stray."

Speaking in soothing terms to a horse, so that he may become familiar to the voice, gives him confidence in his rider, which is of the *utmost importance*. At all times more is to be accomplished with the animal by gentle means than could possibly be done by harsh ones : kindness, or its opposite, is speedily conveyed to and retained in his memory, which is remarkably retentive. This mutual confidence is perfectly appreciated by the Arabs. They invariably treat their horses with the greatest kindness and affection ; they are the Bedouins' beloved and stanch companions, and on them is the Arabs' sole reliance in their predatory excursions; they inhabit the same tent, and the neck of the horse is not unfrequently the pillow of the Arab and his family; yet no accident ever occurs; the kindness with which he is treated gives him an affection for his master, a desire to please, and a pride in exerting every energy in obedience to his command.

Bad habits are speedily acquired by the horse, and when once learned, are very difficult to break him of.

In nine cases out of ten they arise from the *stupidity, joined to the brutality,* of an *idle, drunken, ill-tempered* groom; *who, when out of temper, invariably vents his rage* upon the unoffending animal, which, at last, to protect (or revenge) itself from the besotted tormentor, acquires a habit of kicking and biting at every person and thing coming within its reach, fearing that they are about to maltreat it.

Many horses are condemned as *vicious*, and actually are rendered so through *timidity* on the part of the *rider*.

The animal may be playful from rest, or a lively temper by nature; the rider, *whose judgment* may not enable him to *discriminate* between playfulness, nervousness, or vice, becomes alarmed, and, consesequently, loses his self-command; and, perhaps, not having learned the *correct mode of using* his *hands and reins*, in his *boisterous endeavours* to *save himself from falling*, imparts fear to his horse. The animal naturally imagines he has been guilty of some great fault, and is *fearful of punishment;* and should he *not be familiar with the voice of his rider*, then a mutual struggle for safety takes place, and causes an accident. The horse is *then* condemned as "*vicious*," though the rider was *alone* in fault. The *same horse*, in the hands of an *experienced* horseman, would become as QUIET as ever. We often find that really dangerous horses have been reclaimed by ladies riding them ! This is entirely owing to their using them *gently*, but firmly, and speaking to them kindly ; by these means confidence is imparted, and makes them

"All that a horse should be, which nought did lack
Save a good rider on so proud a back."

A few minutes' riding will be sufficient to discover the nature and temper of a horse, likewise what system of treatment has been pursued towards him (which, in consequence, must be still followed).

There are very many persons who are considered good horsemen, who have no fear, and will ride anything, or *at* anything, yet have no idea, beyond the mere fact of riding, whether the saddle, bridle, and accoutrements are properly placed. The neglect of attending to these matters has caused many serious accidents.

The *method* of gracefully *holding* and *using* the *reins* is *very important*, although but *little under-stood* or *attended* to; in fact, it seems but *a secondary* consideration with Riding-masters, where it should be a SINE QUA NON. One person may pull at a runaway horse with all his strength, but to no purpose; another possessing that knowledge shall be able to manage, and hold him with a pack-thread.

RUNAWAY HORSES are most frequently made so by bad and timid riders, who make use of a whip and spurs without having a *firm seat*. Such persons are easily unseated on the horse shying, or jumping about in a playful mood; then, in their endeavours to recover themselves, they slacken their reins, and at the same time unintentionally goad him with their spurs, or strike him with their whip. In clutching at the reins, the horse becoming frightened, naturally increases his speed, until, from the continued irritation of whip and spur, in the terrified horseman's futile attempts to subdue him, the horse becomes maddened with terror and excitement, and ultimately throws his rider.

SHYING is often the result of skittishness or affectation at first. This may be easily overcome and cured, at its commencement, by the judicious treatment of the rider, in using firmness tempered with kindness; avoiding all harsh measures, and passing the horse several times quietly by the object which caused him to shy. A word, half-scolding, half-encouraging, with a gentle pressure of the heel, or a slight touch of the spur or whip, will convince him there is nothing to fear; and, further, will give the animal *confidence* in his rider on future occasions.

KICKING is a dangerous vice, and generally the result of an idle groom or stable-boy playing with the horse, and pinching him on the loins; so that, should any extraneous substance be in the padding of the saddle, or the flaps of a coat touch him there, or even a hand be thoughtlessly laid on his quarters, he immediately commences kicking to dislodge the cause. Once succeeding, he has invariably recourse to the same remedy, until the habit becomes confirmed.

There are many valuable horses ruined by thoughtlessness and folly.—This is more frequently the case with animals of high courage. In many instances, a *very trivial* alteration in the adjustment of the saddle or bridle, &c. (had the rider been properly instructed, and therefore possessing the knowledge how such alterations should be made), would have saved great danger and annoyance to the rider, and *unnecessary* pain to the horse.

WHEN A HORSE IS KICKING, the rider should throw his body *well back*, raise the horse's head, and apply the whip smartly over his shoulders.

Rearing is very dangerous, and most difficult to break. It is often caused by the bit being too sharp for the horse, his mouth being tender, or perhaps sore.

When rearing, the whole weight of horse and rider being thrown perpendicularly on the animal's hind legs, the *most trifling* check from the rider's hand would cause him to fall backwards; the rider must drop his hand as before, loosen the reins, and throw his whole weight on his shoulders, at the same time catching him 'round the neck with his right hand. These directions will much assist in bringing him down on his feet again, and prevent the rider's body from falling backwards.

Unsteadiness in mounting is very often the consequence of the horse's eagerness and anxiety to start. It is generally the fault with thorough-bred, high-couraged, young and nervous horses. It is a most annoying fault, especially with elderly and timid riders, many of whom are frequently thrown before they can firmly seat themselves.

This is only to be cured by an active and good horseman, combined with firm, though gentle and kind, usage ; by approaching him gently and patting him, mounting at the *first* effort, and when seated, restraining him, patting his neck, and speaking kindly to him, but, at the same time, not allowing him to move until he is perfectly quiet. In a few days he will be quite cured of his fault. Remember! *harshness must never be used* in this case, as great mischief may be done by such a course, and the habit *will be confirmed.*

KINDNESS will succeed generally in most cases of vice ; HARSHNESS *never will* in any !

The position of the saddle should be in accordance with the formation of the horse's shoulders, and about a hand's breadth from them, so as not in any way to interfere with or impede the *free action* of the muscles.

The malposition of the saddle, particularly in horses with upright shoulders, is the cause of many horses falling, from its pressing too much on the shoulders, and by that means confining the action of the muscles, which thus become benumbed, and lose their elasticity. A partial deadening of the limbs having taken place, the horse, from want of vitality

B

in the legs, stumbles, and is unable, through the tor-
pidity of the muscles, to recover himself, and falls
to the ground ; in many cases he has been known to
fall as if shot.

The saddle should be wide, and roomy. The
length of the stirrups should be such as to give ease
to both horse and rider ; the latter ought at all times
to assimilate his movements in the saddle to those
of the horse in his stride.

A tight rein should always be avoided, because,
if he carries his head low, it tends to deaden his
mouth, and teaches him the bad habit of depend-
ing upon the bridle for support ; in which case, he
always goes heavily in hand, and on his shoulders.
The horse should at all times be taught to go on his
haunches.

If the horse naturally carries his head well, it is
better to ride him with a light hand, only just feeling his mouth.

> " With neck like a rainbow, erecting his crest,
>   Pamper'd, prancing, and pleased, his head touching
>   bis breast ;
>   Scarcely snuffing the air, he's so proud and elate,
>   The high-mettled racer first starts for the plate."
>   OLD SONG.

ON PROPERLY FIXING THE BRIDLE, SADDLE, &c.

THE BRIDLE.

In fitting the bridle, THE CURB BIT should be placed so that the mouth-piece be but one inch above the lower tusk,—in mares, two inches above the corner tooth ; THE BRIDOON touching the corner of the lips, so as to fit easy, without wrinkling them ; THE HEADSTALL parallel to the projecting cheek-bone, and behind it ; THE THROAT LASH should be sufficiently long to fall just below the cheek-bone, and not lay over or upon it ; THE NOSE BAND should be placed low—but that must depend very much on the size of the horse's mouth—and not buckled tight; THE CURB, when properly fitted, should be flat and smooth in the hollow of the lips, so as to admit one finger easily between.

THE SADDLE

should be placed in the middle of the horse's back, about a hand's breadth, or four or five inches, from the shoulders, so as to give perfect freedom to the action of the muscles of the shoulders.

THE GIRTHS must be laid evenly one over the other, and admit freedom for one finger between the girth and the horse's belly. THE SURCINGLE should fit neatly over the girths, and not be buckled tighter than they are. The large ring of THE BREASTPLATE or MARTINGALE should be placed about two inches above the sharp breast-bone, and should allow of the hand being laid flat between it and the shoulders.

THE STIRRUPS.

In length they should be so that the bottom edge of the bar is about three inches above the heel of the boot. The author always adopts the following method for ascertaining the correct length of the stirrups, viz.:—He takes up the stirrup-iron with the right hand, at the same time placing the bottom of the stirrup-iron under the left arm-pit, he extends the *left* arm until the fingers of *that* hand *easily touch* the stirrup *buckles; this* is a *sure criterion* with most people.

ON MOUNTING.

In mounting, the horse should always be approached quietly on the near (or left) side, and the reins taken up steadily. THE SNAFFLE (or bridoon) rein first, then pass this rein along the palm of the left hand, between the forefinger and thumb. THE CURB REIN must now be drawn over the little finger, and both reins being held of an equal length, and having an even pressure on the horse's mouth, must be laid over each other, being held firmly in the hand, the thumb pressing hard upon them to prevent them slipping through the fingers. Be particular that the reins are not taken up too short, for fear it might cause the horse to rear or run back ; *they must be held neither too tight nor too slack, but having an equal feeling of the horse's mouth.* Next take up a handful of the mane with the right hand, bring it through the full of the left hand (otherwise the palm), and twist it round the thumb. Take hold of the stirrup with the right hand, the thumb in front. Place the left foot in the stirrup as far as the ball of it, placing the right hand on the cantle (or back part of the saddle), and, by a spring of the right foot from the instep, the rider should raise himself up in the stirrup, then move the hand from the cantle to the pummel, to support the body while the right leg passes clearly over the horse's quarters ; the rider's right knee closes on the saddle and the body falls gently into it. The left hand now quits the mane, and the second stirrup must be taken without the help of eye or hand.

The left hand (the bridle hand) must be placed with the wrist rounded outwards, opposite the centre of the body, and about three inches from it, letting the right arm drop unconstrained by the side of the thigh.

POSITION IN THE SADDLE.

The rider must sit upright, and equally balanced in the middle of his saddle, head erect, and his shoulders well thrown back, his chest advanced, the small of his back bent forward, but without stiffness. The hollow part of the arm should hang down straight from the shoulder, the lower part square to the upper, the thighs well stretched down, the *flat part* to the saddle, so that the fore part of the knees may press and grasp it. Let the legs hang down easily and naturally, close to the horse's sides, with the feet parallel to the same, and the heels well depressed; the toes raised from the instep, and as near the horse's sides as the heels; the feet retained in the stirrups by an easy play of the ankle and stirrup, the stirrup to be kept under the ball of the foot, the joint of the wrist kept easy and pliable, so as to give and take as occasion may require. *A firm and well-balanced position on horseback is of the utmost importance*, it affects the horse in every motion, and failure in this proves one of his greatest impediments, and will naturally injure him in all his movements.

In riding, the hands and legs should act in correspondence in everything, the latter being always held subservient to the former.

It is easy to discover those who have been thoroughly instructed in the *manége*, by their firm, graceful, and uniform position in the saddle, and their ready and skilful application of the aids or motions, and the correct appliance of the bridle, hands, and legs ; such being *indispensable* to the skilful guidance and control of the horse.

PART II.

THE author most particularly wishes to impress upon his readers the value of riding with DOUBLE REINS for safety sake, and in order to avoid the numerous accidents arising from reins breaking, the tongues of buckles giving way, and the sewing of the reins to their bits coming undone. When there is but *one rein*, the rider is left quite at the mercy of an affrighted and infuriated animal; where, had there been TWO, he would still have sufficient command over the animal to prevent accidents.

There is another equally urgent reason for riding with double reins, viz., the continual use of the curb materially tends to deaden the sensitiveness of the horse's mouth; from the constant and unavoidable drag upon the single rein, especially if tender-mouthed, he is made uneasy and fidgetty, causing him to throw his head about, and go extremely heavy in hand, and frequently rear or run back, to the very great danger and annoyance of his rider, particularly when happening in a crowded drive.

It is very requisite to ride a horse occasionally *well up to the curb bit*, and to *keep him well up to it* with the whip and heel, so that he may get used to *work on his haunches.* By this means he will be thrown upon them, and, consequently, "go light in hand," the greater weight being taken from off his forehand, by which his carriage and general appearance is materially improved.

After many essays, the author has found the following method to be the *most correct and* SAFE for holding the reins, when using *one* or *both* hands. By it the rider has a much firmer hold—or, in professional parlance, "purchase"—upon the reins, in keeping them from slipping, consequently, a greater command over the horse, and can more readily allow either rein to slip should he desire to use but one.

FOR HOLDING THE REINS IN ONE HAND.

The reins should hang *untwisted* from the bits.

The rider must take up the bridoon reins with his right hand, and pass the second and third fingers of the bridle, or left, hand between them, draw up the reins with the right hand, until the horse's mouth can be felt, and then pass them between the forefinger and thumb. Next take up the *curb reins* (again with the right hand), and pass the little finger of the bridle hand between them, draw them up, as before directed, with the right hand, until the rider perceives there is an equal length and feeling with the *bridoon* reins. The *latter* having *rather* the strongest pressure on the animal's mouth. This done, *lay them also over* between the forefinger and thumb, and press down the thumb firmly upon them to keep them from slipping; the hand to be held with the wrist rounded outwards, opposite the centre of the body, and about four inches from it.

The right arm should hang without restraint, and *slightly* bent, by the thigh, the whip being held about twelve inches from its head, with the point turned *upwards*.

USING BOTH HANDS.

Take the bridoon reins between the second and third, and the curb reins between the third and fourth, fingers of each hand, each rein having an equal bearing on the horse's mouth; the hands are to be held about six inches apart, with the wrists rounded outwards, and the thumbs pressing firmly upon the reins, the elbows well down, and held near to the sides, the whip held as directed above.

RIDING ON ONE REIN.

Take up THAT particular rein with the right hand, and pass the second and third fingers of the bridle hand between them, then draw up the reins, but be careful, in doing so, not to hold the horse too tight in hand ; the OTHER rein should hang down, having the little finger passed between them, and the thumb also over them, so that they may be caught hold of, and drawn up quickly on any sudden emergency ; the loose reins are to hang between those in use.

THE WHIP.

The whip being a requisite aid in the management and guidance of the horse, should be used as an instrument of correction, and by no means to be *played* with, nor *flourished about.* When using the whip for punishment, *scold* at the same time ; by this means, with a cross word will be associated the idea of chastisement. However, far more can be achieved by kindness than by any harsh measure ; but when such instances occur that it is *absolutely necessary,* never hesitate to *punish well,* so that the animal may thoroughly understand that it is *punishment* that is meant for his fault—*not play.*

" A man of kindness to his beast is kind,
But brutal actions show a brutal mind :
Remember He who made thee, made the brute,
Who gave thee speech and reason, form'd him mute ;
He can't complain, but God's omniscient eye
Beholds thy cruelty. He hears his cry.
He was designed thy servant—not thy drudge ;
But know, that his Creator is thy Judge."

Colt-breaking by the Guachos is performed in the same mode as the Kalmucks, with the lasso; the idea of being thrown, let a horse do what he pleases, never occurs to a Guacho. According to them, a " good rider " is a man who can manage an untamed colt, and one, if his horse should fall, could alight unhurt upon his feet. At the moment of a horse falling backwards they can slip quietly off, and, on the instant of his rising, jump on him again. They never seem to exert muscular force, and appear to ride very loosely, as if every moment they must fall off: yet should his horse be suddenly frightened, the Guacho will start, and take, simultaneously, fright with the horse. There is nothing done on foot by the Guachos that cannot be done on horseback ; even *mounted* beggars are to be seen in the streets of Buenos Ayres and Mendoza. It is not, therefore, surprising that, with such multitudes of horses, that the people should all be riders, and excel all other nations in their expertness and boldness in their management.

The Pampas and Prairie Indians, whose fore-
fathers fled from the Spanish horsemen, as if they
were fatal apparitions, now seem to be part and
parcel of the horse. They affirm the proudest atti-
tude of the human figure is when a man bending
over his horse, lance in hand, is riding *at* his enemy.
The Guachos, who ride so beautifully, declare it is
utterly impossible to vie with mounted Indians;
they have such a way of urging on their horses by
cries, and a peculiar motion of their bodies; even
were they to change horses, the Indians would beat
them.

The Turks prefer the Turkman horse to the
pure-blooded, slender Arabian. In fact, from their
trying mode of riding, the fine limbs of the Arab
could not stand the shock upon them, their favourite
manœuvre being to make a dead stop when gallop-
ing at full speed. To accomplish this feat, they
use a very severe bit, which, of course, destroys
the *sensibility* of their horses' mouths; while, on the
contrary, the Arabs use only a plain snaffle, which
preserves all the sensitiveness of the animals' mouths.

The Toorkman, or Turkman horses.—These are
much esteemed by the Persians. They are large
and swift, and possess extraordinary powers of en-
durance, though they are exceedingly awkward in
appearance. Turkistan is their native region, which

lies north-east of the Caspian Sea ; but their tribes are widely dispersed over Persia, Asia Minor, and Syria.

The Persians are great admirers of horsemanship, and a bad rider affords them infinite amusement. " An officer of an English frigate having gone ashore to visit the envoy, and being mounted on a very spirited horse, and a very bad rider, caused great entertainment to the Persian populace. The next day the man who supplied the ship with vegetables, and spoke a little English, said to the officer, ' Don't be ashamed, sir, nobody knows you — bad rider ! I tell them you, like all English, ride well, but that time they see you very drunk !' We were much amused at this conception of our national character. The Persian thought it would have been *a reproach for a man of a warlike nation not to ride well*, but *none* for a European to get drunk."*

The Syrian horses are reared with the utmost tenderness and care ; they are fondled and played with like children. The Syrian horse is equally good on mountainous, or stony ground, as on the plain ; he is indefatigable, and full of spirit. The Timarli ride horses of the Syrian breed, mostly from their possessing these inestimable qualifications.

* *Vide* " The Horse and his Rider."

C

The Neapolitan horse.—This horse is small, but compact and strong; the head rather large; the neck short, and bull-shaped: the prototype of the horses represented on the bassi-relievi of ancient Roman sculpture. He is capable of living on hard fare, and undergoing great fatigue. He is frequently vicious and headstrong; this is chiefly owing to his harsh treatment; though very high-spirited, he would, with gentle usage, become extremely docile and good tempered. The districts of Apulia, Abruzzi, and parts of Calabria furnish this excellent animal. The Neapolitans have taken extreme pains in the breeding of their horses; they make great display of them in their streets during the Carnival, and through Lent. The aristocratic families have excellent studs of great spirit and beauty.

PART III.

ON THE PACES OF THE HORSE.

THE WALK.

Of all the paces, the walk is the easiest to the rider, *provided* he sits in the centre of his horse's back, as it consists of an alternate depression of the fore and hind quarters.

The motion may be compared to the vibration of the beam of a pair of scales. The walk should be light, firm, and quick ; the knee must be moderately bent, the leg should appear suspended in the air for an instant, and the foot fall perfectly flat to the ground.

It is very difficult to confine young and mettle some horses to a walk ; great good temper, with a firm light hand, are requisite to accomplish this. When such horses change to a trot they should be *stopped for a minute* or two, and *then* allowed to proceed again. If the animal carries his head well, ride him with a moderately loose rein, raising the hand when he tries to break into a trot.

THE TROT.

The trot is allowed, by professionals, to be the only just basis upon which equestrians can ever attain a secure and graceful seat, combined with confidence and firmness. The rider has more control over the motions of his body in this pace than any other: in this the body is well brought down into the saddle by its own weight, and finds its true equilibrium. When the rider wishes to make his horse trot, let him ease his reins and press the calves of his legs gently ; when his horse is at a trot, let him feel both his reins, raise his horse's forehand, and keep his haunches well under him.

THE CANTER.

The rider must have a light and firm feeling of both reins to raise his horse's forehand ; at the same time, with a pressure of both calves, to bring the animal's quarters well under him, having a double feeling of the inward rein, and a strong pressure of the outward leg, to cause him to strike off in unison.

At all times the horse should be taught to lead off with EITHER fore leg ; by doing so his legs will not be so much shaken, especially the off fore leg, which is the one he most generally leads off on. This must be the case when he is *continually throwing* the greater part of his weight upon the leading fore leg, as it comes to the ground, which causes lameness of the foot, and strains the back sinews of the legs. Being thoroughly taught to change his legs, the horse is better enabled to perform long journeys, with facility and comfort both to himself and his rider.

TURNING.

In the turn either to the right or left, the reins must be held quite evenly, so that the horse may be immediately made to feel the aid of the rider's hands; he (the rider) must then have a double feeling on the inward rein, also retaining a steady feeling on the *outward;* the horse being kept up to the hand by a pressure of both legs, the outward leg being the stronger.

REINING BACK.

The rider should frequently practise reining back, which is of the utmost service both to himself and his horse : by it, the rider's hand is rendered firm and materially strengthened ; and the pliancy of wrist so essential to the complete management of the horse is achieved, likewise causing the body of the rider to be well thrown back and his chest expanded, thus forcing, and preserving, an *erect* position in the saddle. Also, the *carriage* of the horse becomes greatly improved ; his head is maintained in its correct position, and he is compelled to work correctly on his haunches.

In "reining back," the horseman requires a light and steady feeling of both reins, a pressure of both legs, so as to raise his horse's forehand and keep his haunches *well under* him, at the same time *easing* the reins, and *feeling them again* after every step.

STOPPING.

None are thoroughly taught until quite AU FAIT in the stop. It is of *far greater importance* than may be *usually* imagined. In the first place, it shows the horse to be *well under* COMMAND, especially when the rider is able to do so *instantaneously :* it saves in the second place, many serious and inevitable accidents from carriages, horsemen, &c., such as crossing before suddenly pulling up, turning quickly round a corner, or coming unawares upon the rider.

Care must be taken to make the STOP *steadily ; not* by a *sudden jerk* upon the *bit ;* by doing so the horse, if "tender mouthed," will be made to rear and plunge. To make the horse stop properly, the bridle-hand must be kept low, and the knuckles turned down. The rider's body must be well thrown back ; he must have a steady feeling of both reins, and, *closing* both legs for a moment, so keep his horse well up to hand. N. B.—The rider's hands always must be eased as soon as halted.

LEAPING.

Much depends upon the manner of bringing a horse up to the leap ; he should be taken up straight and steady to it, with the reins held in each hand— they must be kept low, with the *curb*-rein held loosely. The rider's body should be kept erect, pliant, and easy in its movements. As the animal is in the act of rising in his leap and coming again to the ground, the rider's body must be well thrown back.

The sitting of a leap, *well*, is entirely dependent upon the proper balance of the body ; thereby the weight is thrown correctly into the saddle, and thus *meets* the horse's movements.

THE STANDING LEAP.

Let the rider take up his horse at an animated pace, halt him with a light hand upon his haunches ; when rising at the leap, the rider should only just feel the reins, so as to prevent them becoming slack, when he springs forward, yielding them without reserve ; as, at the time, the horse must be left quite at liberty. As the horse's hind feet come to the ground, the rider must again collect him, resume his usual position, and move on at the same pace. His body must be inclined forward as the horse rises, and backwards as he alights.

FLYING LEAP.

The horse must not be hurried, but taken up at a brisk pace, with a light and steady hand, keeping his head perfectly steady and straight to the bar or fence. This position is the same as in the standing leap; and the aids required are the same as for making a horse canter.

If held too tight in the act of leaping, the horse is likely to overstrain himself, and fall. If hurried at a leap, it may cause him to miss his distance, and spring too soon, or too late; therefore his pace must be regulated, so that he may take his spring distant enough, and proportionate to its height, so that he may clear it.

When nearing the leap the rider must sit perfectly square, erect, pliant, and easy in the act of leaping; on arriving at the opposite side of the leap, throw the body well back, and again have the horse well in hand.

SWIMMING A HORSE.

The rider must take up and cross his stirrups, which will prevent the horse from entangling himself or his rider; should he commence plunging and struggling in the water, *then quite* loosen the *curb-*

reins, and scarcely feel the bridoon ; any attempt to guide the horse must be made by the slightest touch of the rein possible.

The rider also must have his chest as much over the horse's withers as he can, and throw his weight forward, holding on by the mane, to prevent the rush of water from carrying him backwards.

Should a horse appear distressed, a person unable to swim may, with great safety, hold firmly by the mane, and throw himself out flat on the water ; by those means he relieves the animal from his weight, and the horse coming once more into his depth, the rider may again recover his position in the saddle.

BOLTING, OR RUNNING AWAY.

This dangerous habit is to be found very generally in nervous and young horses, who at the least noise, become alarmed, and try to escape ; quickening their pace, they break from a trot to a gallop, until terrified with the impotent struggles of their riders to stop them, or the sound of wheels behind them, they become maddened, and dash on in their perilous career.

Once a horse finds he has succeeded in these efforts, on any recurrence of noise or cause of affright, he will pursue the same course, to the imminent peril of life, limb,—not only of the rider or driver,—but of whoever or whatever he may chance to meet in his impetuous flight. The habit at length becomes confirmed, and it is alone by the utmost nerve and coolness, tempered with firmness and kindness, that we may hope eventually to overcome the disease.

When a horse is known to have a disposition for running away, a firm, steady hold should be kept over him, at the same time speaking soothingly and encouragingly; but, at the least symptom, checking sharply and scolding him, and never allowing him to increase his pace of his own accord, as fear will oftentimes cause him at length to break into a gallop.

Either in riding or driving, the reins should be held firmly, and the horse had well in hand; but not by a constant pull to deaden the sensitiveness of his mouth ; taking care occasionally to ease the reins and keep the mouth alive by a gentle motion of the bit, only just loosening them, so that on any symptom of running away or bolting, they may be caught up quickly, and the horse be well placed under command, without frightening him.

By a little judicious management in this way, with patience, kindness tempered with firmness, a cure in most cases will be completed in a short time.

In riding and driving horses addicted to running away, be *very particular* that all portions of the horse furniture be sound and strong, more *especially the reins* and BITS.

PART IV.

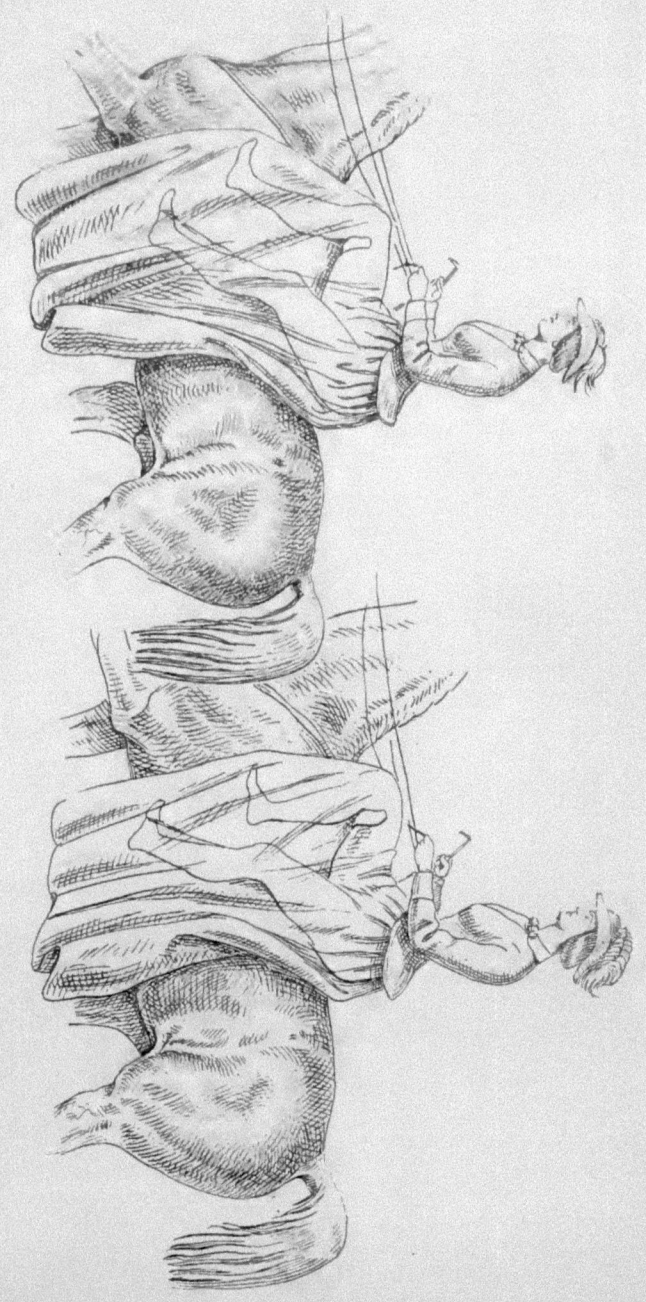

ADVICE TO LADIES.

PREPARATORY to a lady mounting her horse, she should carefully approach to the shoulder. The quietest animal will sometimes kick on a person coming suddenly to him from behind ; but if neared in the manner described, he cannot possibly contrive to bite or kick.

It is also correct to allow the horse to see his rider as much as possible, as it obviates the fright occasioned by a person getting suddenly on his back, that he has not previously seen coming to him.

THE HABIT.

Both the habit and *under* garments should be full, as upon this so much depends the requisite ease and graceful appearance. The habit should not, however, be too long, as it is liable to become entangled in the horse's legs. Sometimes serious and even fatal falls have occurred from this cause, particularly if the horse falls to the ground, as the habit cannot be speedily extricated from under him.

The author here strongly advises a lady *never* to tuck her skirts tight over the crutch of her

D

saddle, but take pains to have them so easy, as to be enabled on the instant to disengage *both* skirts and knee. A facility, *in this*, can only be acquired by *constant* practice ; and it is of far greater importance to the lady equestrian to attain, than may appear at the first glance. Had this *apparently slight* attainment been made a matter of *moderate* consideration, many a parent need not have had to deplore the *death or disfigurement* of a beloved child.

When a lady has her habit drawn over the crutch of her saddle, and tucked tightly in under her leg (for the purpose of keeping the skirt in its proper position), she denies herself the full liberty of her knee, and in case of accident, to be off the horse.

On the slightest warning, though *foreseen*, whatever the danger, the *tightness* of the lady's dress will not allow her to get her leg out of its place, in time to make any effectual effort to save herself ; also, it is probable that the habit might get entangled in the pummel, and she, frightened of course, would become unable to disengage her foot from the stirrup (or shoe), in which case she inevitably experiences the most appalling of all accidents,—*being dragged powerless, by a terrified horse, a considerable distance along the road.*

Before closing this portion of his subject, the author is rejoiced that the extremely dangerous and most unnecessary fashion of wearing " Habit Brooches" is now no longer adopted,—things solely invented for "trade purposes,"—and to any, and especially to a graceful horsewoman, a truly ridiculous article to wear : never to be patronized by a lady, anxious for her own safety and the feelings of her family and friends.

To illustrate this :—The position of a lady on horseback is greatly limited, when compared to that a gentleman ; necessarily then, when her skirt is confined by a " Habit Brooch," *all power* must be taken away, and *all chance* of escape, when an accident occurs. A *very* slight fall to the lady may be fatal, where, had she had the full liberty of her skirt, it would have been very trivial. The *proper* arrangement of the skirt of the riding-dress, to prevent its flying about, entirely depends on the lady herself.

MOUNTING.

Two persons are absolutely necessary to assist a lady to mount ; one to keep the horse quiet, by standing in front of him, and holding the reins close to the bit, *one rein in each hand ;* the other is for assisting her to mount. The lady, having regulated her habit, must stand perfectly erect; her right hand, having the bridoon-rein hanging loosely on the thumb, being placed upon the upright horn of the saddle (her whip held between the thumb and forefinger), her right side towards and close to it.

The second person, who is to assist the lady to mount, must now place himself near to, and almost fronting her; having united his hands by putting his fingers between each other, and stooping down near to the ground, receives the lady's left foot, which should be placed firmly in them, care being previously taken that no part of her skirt is under it. The left knee should be kept as straight as possible, in order to give additional purchase, while lifting her perpendicularly and gracefully into the saddle. The lady must then place her left hand on his right shoulder, and as he lifts her, *she must spring from the instep*, at the same time guiding herself into the saddle with her right hand.

Having gained her saddle, the lady should take hold of her habit with her right hand, close to the knee, and raise it sufficiently to allow of the right knee dropping *well home* into the crutch, and keeping it there, as far as she possibly can, immovable.

RULES FOR GAINING THE CORRECT POSITION IN THE SADDLE.

Before a lady mounts she must endeavour to carry in her mind's eye the *centre* of her saddle. On *this centre* she must, as nearly as possible, place herself; and to assist her memory, she should take it for a rule, to keep her eyes in a straight line between the horse's ears when lifted into it. By these means, after a little practice, she will not fail to drop almost insensibly into the correct position ; the weight of her body being thrown full into the centre of the saddle, rendering her seat firm and easy to her horse and herself. For example :— should we place a weight on one side of a table, the other side having nothing on it as a balance; if it does not actually fall, it will become extremely insecure and unsteady ; but, on the contrary, if the weight be placed in the centre, the table will be safe and steady, even if ricketty before ; therefore, if the lady does not sit "square" (that is, quite in the centre) on her horse, she must inevitably throw all her weight to one side, and thereby destroy her power over the horse, and instead of giving him his correct action, render him unsafe, and shambling in his gait.

THE POSITION IN THE SADDLE.

To obtain a correct position in the saddle, the lady must keep her head erect, and her shoulders well thrown back, which will have the effect of expanding the chest, and giving the requisite hollowness to the small of the back. It is also most important that the rider should keep her body from the waist to the bust very easy, in no way to be constrained, more especially across the loins. By observing these directions, the lady will be enabled to accommodate herself, without uneasiness, to the motions of her horse.

When the upper portion of the body regulates itself by its *elasticity* to the paces of the horse, there is this additional advantage,—let the animal plunge or struggle as it may, if the rider keeps her knee immovable in its place, her left foot in the stirrup (with the toe turned in, which eminently assists her seat and balance), and preserves her presence of mind, and overcomes any approach to nervousness, she cannot be unseated.

THE ARMS.

They should hang *perfectly* independent of the body, from the shoulders near the sides, *yet quite* free from having a constrained appearance.

THE LEGS.

The right leg from the hip to the knee should be kept down in the saddle, and, as much as the rider possibly can, without moving. The lady will materially assist herself in this object by drawing *the heel backwards*. The left leg must hang steady, *yet* not, by any means, rest its weight in the stirrup, for in consequence of the muscles of the leg being round, the foot will naturally turn outward, thus causing a wavering, tottering seat, inclining the body too much out of balance, and giving a disunited motion to the horse, and an ungraceful and deformed appearance to the rider. To prevent this, the knee must be kept firmly pressed to the saddle ; and, as before remarked, by depressing the heel, the toe will be naturally turned in.

THE STIRRUP.

The position of the foot in the stirrup is of great importance ; upon it depends much ; keeping the correct balance of the body on the horse, which consists in sitting perfectly square and erect, and preserving a steady position in the saddle. In fitting the stirrup the lady ought to have her length correctly arranged, which is done in the following manner:—The stirrup leg must hang quite free from the hip-joint, the knee being slightly bent, with the toes raised and turned in towards the horse's side. Keep the foot fixed as immovable as possible in the stirrup, allowing the pressure alone to come from the toes to the bridge of the foot, which will have the effect of giving the elasticity and regularity of movement required in the horse's quickened paces.

The *length* of the stirrup must be made a matter of importance. On it, in a very great measure, *depends* a steady, firm seat.

THE STIRRUP TOO LONG.

In the lady's endeavours to retain her foot in the stirrup, her weight must preponderate on the left side; if the stirrup be *too short*, it necessarily gives a rolling motion to her body, destructive alike to grace, elegance, and security of seat, and will prevent her seating herself sufficiently back in her saddle.

THE BRIDLE HAND.

The motion of the lady's hand must be confined to the *wrist*—as in pianoforte playing—the action coming from *it alone*.

By the management of the reins, in concert with the yielding or retraction of the wrists, the horse is guided in his paces. By this mode the sensibility and goodness of his mouth is preserved ; the beauty of his action is developed ; steadiness is combined with security in his paces, and the safety of his rider is secured. The degree of command, which the animal can be placed under, *entirely depends on the degree of proficiency* acquired in this branch.

GUIDING.

There are *four* motions requisite in guiding a horse.

To go forward.—Lengthen the reins, and give the animal his liberty. For this purpose the lady's hand must be guided by the *action* of her wrist, and, at the same time, she must apply gently her whip. Here, it is proper to remark, the lady's bridle, or left, hand must never be left inactive, but, by practice, she must endeavour to understand the art of *feeling the horse's mouth;* should the bridle hand *not* be kept in constant use this will never come easy to the rider, the hand will be unsteady, and the horse will become the same.

To go backward.—The reins must be shortened a little, the back of the hand turned down, the little finger next the body ; the weight of the rider should be thrown back, with the little finger slightly pulled in towards the waist, then the horse will readily step back.

To turn to the right.—The hand must be turned upwards, which will direct the little finger to the right. Throw the balance of the body into the turn, by inclining the bust to the right and applying the whip, which will cause the horse to move forward as he turns, obey the hand, and cross his legs one over the other, correctly.

To turn to the left.—Let the hand be turned down, so that the little finger may be directed to the left ; the bust must also be turned to the left, and the hand up, with the left heel applied to his side, and the whip to his right shoulder.

DISMOUNTING.

There is tact necessary in dismounting, in order that the lady may avoid the *exposé* and inelegance, attendant upon, as it were, being lifted from the saddle in a groom's arms.

Previous to dismounting, the groom must stand by the horse's head, holding the reins close to the bit, to keep him as steady as possible.

The lady having removed her foot from the stirrup, and passed her hand down to free her skirt, etc., from all chance of catching to the saddle or stirrup, should remove her knee out of the crutch ; at the same time taking the precaution to disengage the habit from that side. Then holding the crutch with her right hand (the rein hanging loosely on the thumb), and now placing her left hand on her groom's right arm, near the wrist ; his arm being extended for the purpose, she must spring lightly and clear from the saddle, slightly inclining the bust towards the horse's shoulder.

By this method the lady will quite disengage herself, and descend gently to the ground.

MAXIMS TO BE ATTENDED TO.

Be particular to avoid nervousness and hurry, either in mounting or dismounting.

Take time, and have everything correctly arranged before starting ; serious accidents have occurred frequently from being in haste to start off.

Arrange the habit, length of stirrup, and have the saddle-bands and buckles properly examined before the journey is begun, to prevent having to stop on the road.

Be careful to keep the hand active, and watch the movements of the horse ; by this means the rider will never be thrown off her guard, and will be prepared for every emergency.

Keep the horse's mouth always in play, so as to keep up its fine feeling, *indispensable* to his correct guidance.

Never allow the reins to hang loosely on the horse's neck, crutch, or pummel of the saddle. This oversight frequently causes serious and fatal accidents.

Always use *double* reins. Should one become useless, there is still another to rely upon.

Before the author concludes, he begs to be allowed to *impress* upon his fair readers, that an *elegant* and accomplished *equestrian* becomes an equally *graceful pedestrian*, from the improved carriage acquired from proficiency in the former accomplishment.

To become an *elegant pedestrian* is no mean task, nor is it an *easy* one to accomplish. Yet it is of the utmost importance to a lady, *in particular*, to master it. How often, in our experience through life, have we met with a lovely face and perfect figure,— everything that could constitute the perfection of female beauty, *while at rest!*—but once in *motion*, the illusion is dispelled from a *bad carriage and shuffling gait*, the perfect form becomes quite common-place. These two destructives to beauty can be entirely eradicated by attention to the following directions, and which apply equally to

WALKING AND RIDING.

Keep the bust and head *erect;* the shoulders *well thrown back.* The motive power to proceed from the hips *alone.*

Perseverance in these few directions will soon give all that is required for a graceful and healthy carriage.

Finally.—At all times *trust to your reins for security,* in cases of danger. *Never* grasp the pummel of the saddle. Never use a " Habit Brooch."

REMARKS ON SADDLERY.

I HAVE been quite surprised to see, in such a city as London, the paucity of really good saddles. Most of them would disfigure any horse they were put upon, with flaps of all shapes but the right.

To say how a saddle should be made, would be quite impossible, as it solely depends on the horse and his rider ; for instance, a thin and sweepy saddle will not suit a horse with round, heavy shoulders, and wide over his loins. Many imagine that cut-back saddles are less liable to injure the rider, than ordinary ones ; this is quite fallacious.

The saddle must have the head, or what is called, the pummel, to begin upon ; and the further *that* can be carried forward the better ; but the nearer it is got under the seat, the more likely is it *to seriously injure* the rider.

In *side*-saddles there is great variety ; but the requisites for a *first-rate* side-saddle, to my idea, and one I would not hesitate in recommending, should be *length* (*indispensable*), *a leaping-head*, *no off-*

head, and it should be cut as nearly level as possible. None, I may say, can dispute my first remark, and *none* who have ridden with the leaping-head will ever after be *without it.*

There are those who say no, to the off-head being cut away, " for should a lady become nervous, she could not steady herself so well as if the head had been left on ;" here I fully agree, but beg to say in reply, that before a lady attempts the road or anywhere where she might be placed in such a critical position, she must have her nerves so strengthened through her equestrian education, that she need not look to the off-head of her saddle for safety ; her *point d'appui is* the leaping-head. When holding on by the off-head, the lady of course loses *the use* of one hand. Next, her horse may go where he pleases, for she cannot get her hands down to have a good pull at his mouth. Then, in hunting, the poor lady's wrists are everlastingly bruised by the off-head, to say nothing of the danger of their being broken by it.

BRIDLES.

There is a great variety of bridles. Generally speaking, the plainer the bridle the better, more especially for hunting and hacking ; for the former, let your bit be long in the cheek (*i.e.*, in moderation), the mouth-piece thick, having the bridoon the same, the *suaviter in modo* being much more agreeable than the *fortiter in re*, to all animals. For hack bridles, any fancy cheek may do, if the horse's head be sufficiently handsome ; but let me request my readers not to put a fancy bridle on a coarse-bred, common horse.

THE THROAT LASH.

Simple as it may appear, it spoils the heads of all horses, as it is usually made. It should be long enough to fall just below the cheek-bone, and not to lay *on* or *over* it, as it makes the animal's head look short and thick.

NOSE BAND.

Not as they were used in days past, *attached* to bridle, but *separate*. No one knows its efficacy when placed low, but those who have tried it ; its exact position will, of course, depend much on the size of the mouth.

CHIN STRAP.

Some imagine this is not an indispensable thing to a bridle, either in hunting or hacking, *but it*

E

is, more especially in *Pelham's.* I have seen a horse in tossing his head, throw the Pelham bit over on to his face; had a chin strap been attached to the bridle, this could not have happened.

THE EQUESTRIAN'S MANUAL.

(Dedicated to H.R.H. Prince Albert.)

BY S. C. WAITE, ESQ.

OPINIONS OF THE PRESS.

Standard.

MR. WAITE's book will put *every one*, who shall obey its instructions, in the way of riding *well;* for it does as much as a book can to teach the theory of the art. It is a book to be purchased and carefully read by every one, not an experienced horseman, who purposes to ride or buy a horse, and even the *experienced* horseman will find in it *valuable* information.

Morning Advertiser.

THIS work reflects high credit on Mr. Waite for its practical lucidity, and the pleasing manner in which the instructions are imparted. His directions for *curing* the acquired *bad* habits of horses, too often the results of ill usage, or violence of ignorant grooms and horse-breakers, are excellent. The position of the saddle, the proper fixing of it and the bridle, the *best* method of mounting, position in the saddle (illustrated by diagrams), are carefully and sensibly treated on. The third section, "Advice to Ladies," is novel, and the hints *invaluable, not only to the fair sex, but to those who may have to instruct them in the graceful art of Equitation.*

Morning Chronicle.

IN bringing under notice a new book, practical and highly amusing, upon the noble Art of Horsemanship, which has emanated from the pen of a well-known and accomplished professor thereof, we have pleasure in stating the reader will find in these pages excellent practical hints and sound suggestions on the art of riding well; and, in the manner of training and treating horses we sincerely concur with, and we honour and respect Mr. Waite, when he so forcibly inculcates kindness and gentleness, though combined with firmness, as essentials in the education and treatment of the horse; hardships, cruelty, and neglect he strongly deprecates.

The instructions in the proper seat and carriage on horseback, the management of the whip and rein, are minutely explained, and of the greatest utility. He is particularly attentive to the ladies, and admitting the power they lose by their peculiar seat, he gives the best recommendations for remedying the evil, as far as possible, by securing an exactly central fix upon the saddle, the best form of which he learnedly discusses. Speaking seriously, all fair riders ought, for their own sake, to profit by his advice, the result of long experience.

Sunday Times.

Mr. WAITE, an *experienced professor* of the art, has given us a hand-book, *in which* will be found a great variety of instruction, by which the equestrian will receive such directions for the management of his horse, under a variety of circumstances, as must prove of *great value* to him.

Observer.

THIS work is *evidently* the production of one who has acquired a *thorough* acquaintance with the subject, and who, moreover, possesses the *rare advantage* of communicating his instructions in a manner peculiarly *ample* and *clear*. We have seen *no* other work in which such a variety of information on the subject is embraced. The advice to ladies is most valuable.

MR. S. C. WAITE,

AUTHOR OF "THE EQUESTRIAN'S MANUAL,"

(*Dedicated to H.R.H. Prince Albert,*)

With advice to purchasers of Horses, &c., and Originator of the Improved Military Seat (obviating ruptures), and positions for Ladies and Gentlemen on Horseback.—(Vide *Opinions of the Press, April,* 1850.)

MR. WAITE has been requested by a numerous circle of personal friends to submit to the notice of the public an ointment, proved to be invaluable to the owners of racing and hunting establishments, breeders, farmers, &c., for restoring hair on broken knees, and where it has been lost, through accidents, disease, blistering, firing, &c., &c.; it is likewise available for dogs in reproducing hair, bare from mange, scalds, burns, and abrasions.

Mr. Waite obtained the above valuable recipe from the late celebrated and eccentric character, Patrick Jones, of Dublin, familiarly known in military and sporting circles, and throughout the kingdom, as "Old Paddy," who, after an unfailing success in its use, in all parts of the world (where called by his military duties), for a period verging on eighty years (and by him obtained from his father), on his death-bed, in 1853, confided the secret to the present proprietor.

To be had in pots at 3s., 5s., 8s., and 17s. 6d., and in 8lb. canisters for hounds after mange, &c., &c., at £4. 4s.

TESTIMONIALS.

From Dr. Bunting, *the great American Horse Tamer and Breaker.*

2, Onslow Terrace, Brompton,
May 22nd, 1859.

Sir,—I beg to certify that I have used your "Old Paddy Jones's Ointment" for restoring hair on horses and dogs, in *numerous* cases of valuable horses, and in *no instance* has it failed in its efficacy, and I consider it to be invaluable to every establishment where horses and dogs are kept. In future, I shall never be without it. Wishing you every success,

Believe me to be truly yours,

J. G. Bunting.

S. C. Waite, Esq.,
Brompton.

Patent American Break Office,
Mason's Riding School, Brompton,
July 7th, 1859.

Sir,—Having used your "Old Paddy Jones's Ointment" for restoring the hair on horses and dogs, I have great pleasure in testifying to its *good* qualities in all the cases I have had in hand, and think it will be a *great boon* to all keeping either a horse or dog.

I remain, Sir,

Yours obediently,

To S. C. Waite, Esq.,   Henry Hurst.
Brompton.

ROBERT HARDWICKE, PRINTER, 192, PICCADILLY.